# To the POST OFFICE

## with Mama

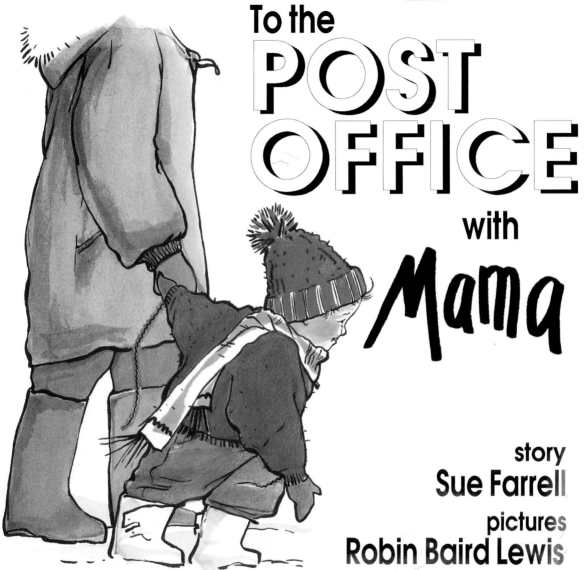

story
**Sue Farrell**

pictures
**Robin Baird Lewis**

**ANNICK PRESS LTD.**
Toronto ● New York

Second printing, November 1995

Annick Press Ltd.

Annick Press gratefully acknowledges the support of the
Canada Council and the Ontario Arts Council.

**Canadian Cataloguing in Publication Data**
Farrell, Sue.
  To the post office with Mama

ISBN 1-55037-359-5 (bound). - ISBN 1-55037-358-7 (pbk.)
I. Lewis, Robin Baird. II. title.

PS8561.A77T6 1994   jC813'.54   C93-095218-9
PZ7.F37To 1994

The art in this book was rendered in markers and watercolours.
The text was typeset in Nebraska.

Distributed in Canada by:
Firefly Books Ltd.
250 Sparks Avenue
Willowdale, ON
M2H 2S4

Published in the U.S.A. by Annick Press (U.S.) Ltd.
Distributed in the U.S.A. by:
Firefly Books (U.S.) Inc.
P.O. Box 1338
Ellicott Station
Buffalo, NY 14205

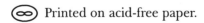 Printed on acid-free paper.

Printed and bound in Canada by
Friesens, Altona, Manitoba.

I am going to the post office with Mama.
It's cold outside.

I put on my coat, my boots, my hat and my mittens. My thumb goes in a special place all by itself.

I open the door
and jump outside.

I kick the snow
with my boots.

Here comes the bus.
I wave to the driver.
She makes the horn go "beep, beep,"
and she waves back to me.

The snow is piled very high beside the sidewalk.
I can't see the cars and trucks anymore,
but I can hear their motors.

I look for a snowman, but all I can see
are the tops of trees.

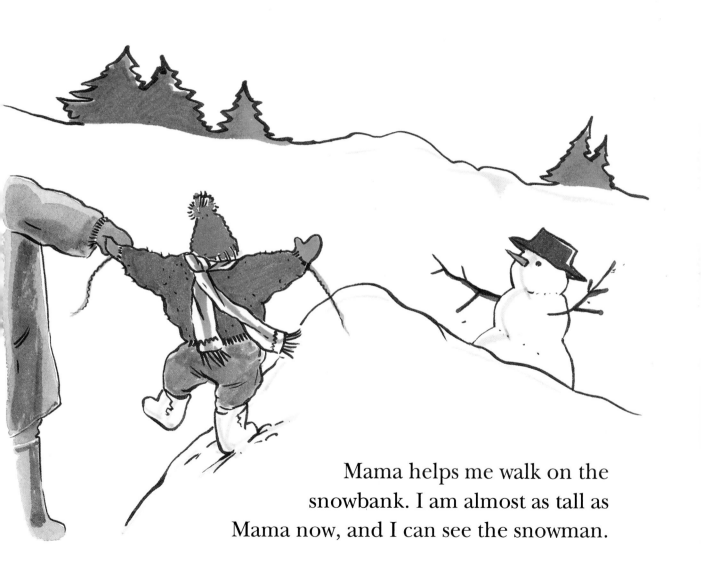

Mama helps me walk on the
snowbank. I am almost as tall as
Mama now, and I can see the snowman.

When we pass the church, I run away
from Mama and climb the steps. Mama
says, "No, Shea. Come this way."

I run past Mama. She swings her arms like my dancing monkey puppet and chases me.

She says, "Agghh," in a scary voice.
I giggle and run faster.

We are nearly at the post office.

I can see the train now. The train makes loud
noises and its wheels go around and around.

I wave to the train. It goes, "toot, toot, toot."

Beside the Town Office is a big, green
garbage can where I put candy
wrappers and banana peels.

I stand on my tippy-toes to look inside.
There are no wrappers or
banana peels – only snow.

There is the place where grown-ups wash clothes.

I clean the snow off a bench. I stand up on the seat to look at the woman inside. Her clothes are going around and around in the dryer.

"Hurry up, Shea. Come this way," says Mama.

I can see the post office now.

It is my favourite building. It has a ramp for
people with wheelchairs. In the summer I pull my
wagon down the ramp. In winter I run down very fast.

Inside, the post office has a metal door where I
mail letters to Nanny. I stretch as tall as I can
and pull the handle. Mama drops the letter in the
door and the mailman will bring it to Nanny next week.

The post office has a place where the mailman
leaves letters for Mama and me.

Mama gives me the key to open our mailbox. I push in
the key and turn it. The little door opens and Mama
takes out our letters. I try to open other mailboxes.
"No, Shea," Mama says. "It's time to go."

I push open the glass door and run down the ramp
as fast as I can.

At the bottom, Mama takes my hand.
We start to walk home.

But I am getting tired of walking. "I'm sleepy," I say. Mama picks me up and kisses me.

I lay my head on Mama's shoulder. The fur on her parka tickles my face. I close my eyes and go to sleep.

Mama carries me home.

I wake up when she takes off my coat,
my boots, my hat and my mittens.

She lays me on my bed and covers me with
my special blanket and whispers,
"Sleep well, baby."

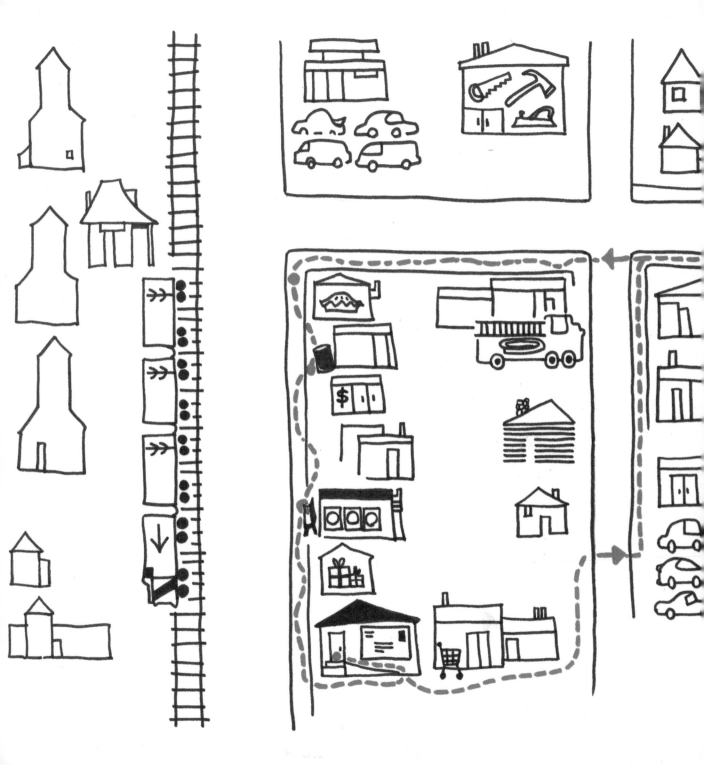

JE
Farrell, Sue
To the post office with Mama
15.95